A Day in the Life of La Gatita de Oro in Apt. 6-J

Salsa Dancing

Written by Ivette Méndez
Illustrated by Carlos Luis Méndez

Dedicated to our parents . . .
Inés and Roberto

La Gatita de Oro, also known as Miss Kitty, is the inspiration for our book, which takes place in the author's apartment in Montclair, New Jersey.

"¡Adiós my Gatita de Oro!
I'm off to work.
Don't spend the whole day
sleeping and eating.
Try to get some exercise."

"EXERCISE?
I'd rather eat my treats
and take my cat naps
and then wake up to
eat my treats some more.
¡Qué rico!"

And besides,
La Gatita de Oro wondered,
what kind of exercise
can a cat do?

"I know! I can ask
Robertito and Inesita
who live in the nest in the tree
outside my window."

"Amiguitos, I'm
just a simple gata
who likes to take cat naps
and eat my treats.

Can you tell me
what kind of
exercise a gata
like me can do?"

"Gatita de Oro,
the answer is quite simple,"
replied Robertito.

"Salsa dancing!" exclaimed Inesita.

"Salsa dancing?
Why, that's a great idea!"

So La Gatita de Oro
padded over to
the shiny silver radio
and gently pressed a button
on the remote.

And salsa music
poured into
the apartment!

La Gatita de Oro
began to move.

♪

And, caramba, did she move!

As the sounds of
congas and bongós
and timbales
filled the air . . .

La Gatita de Oro
jumped with joy
here and there!

She was twisting and turning and flinging her front paws into the air.

She twirled on the couch
and on the table . . .

And into the kitchen

where she grabbed a few
treats without missing
any beats.

And then,
shaking her bottom,
she danced down
the long hallway
and into
the bedroom.

"I love salsa dancing!"
La Gatita de Oro exclaimed
as she jumped on the bed.

"But I'd rather eat my treats
and take my naps
and then wake up
to eat my treats some more!"

And so
La Gatita de Oro
curled up
and went to sleep.

"Oh you spent
another day sleeping
and eating.

So I see that I will
have to come up with
a new idea for a day
in the life of
La Gatita de Oro!"

About the Author and Illustrator

Ivette and Carlos come from a family of nine sisters and brothers. Their parents, Inés and Roberto Méndez, moved from Puerto Rico, where Ivette was born, to Washington D.C., where Carlos was born two years after his sister. The family eventually relocated to Plainfield, New Jersey, where Ivette and Carlos grew up.

Ivette has loved to read and write since she was a little girl. She spent many happy hours at the Plainfield Public Library throughout her childhood picking out books that she would read from early morning to late at night.

Ivette wrote for school newspapers while attending Maxson Junior High School (now Middle School), Plainfield High School, and Douglass College in New Brunswick, New Jersey. She was a reporter at two daily newspapers in New Jersey.

Carlos has held a pencil, a crayon or a brush for as long as he can remember. His father bought him his first set of oil paints when he was 12. Through the years, he has continued to create artwork while maintaining a full-time job.

Published by Page Turning Books

an imprint of

Turn the Page Publishing LLC
P. O. Box 3179
Upper Montclair, NJ 07043
www.turnthepagepublishing.com

ISBN: 978-1-938501-57-9

A Day in the Life of LaGatita de Oro in Apt. 6J
Salsa Dancing

Library of Congress Control Number: 2014951255

CPSIA Section 103(a) Compliant

Printed in the United States of America

Page Turning Books
an imprint of
TurnthePagePublishing.com

CPSIA information can be obtained at www.ICGtesting.com
Printed in the USA
BVOW10*0608171114

375414BV00002B/1/P